In the Time Travel Secrets Series:

Moneyline Secrets
Family Secrets

Family Secrets

by R.W. Wallace

Copyright © 2021 by R.W. Wallace

Cover by the author

Cover Illustration 459254108 © Thurgood | depositphotos.com

Cover Illustration 11106798 © Hannamariah | depositphotos.com

All characters and events in this book, other than those clearly in the public domain, are fictitious and any resemblance to real persons, living or dead, is purely coincidental.

All rights reserved. No part of this publication may be reproduced, distributed, or transmitted in any form or by any means, including photocopying, recording, or other electronic or mechanical methods, without the prior written permission of the publisher, except in the case of brief quotations embodied in critical reviews and certain other noncommercial uses permitted by copyright law. For permission requests, write to the publisher, addressed "Attention: Permissions Coordinator," at the address below.

www.rwwallace.com

ISBN: [979-10-95707-79-0]

Main category—Fiction

Other category—Time Travel

First Edition

R.W. WALLACE

Author of the Ghost Detective Series

FAMILY SECRETS

A Time Travel Secrets Short Story

One

Rose slid off the wagon and collapsed in a relieved heap on the dusty ground, her back against the spokes of the wheel and a stone biting into her already sore behind. She didn't even care. The stone had nothing on the hard bench she'd been bouncing on for countless weeks and it had the incredible advantage of *not moving*.

As her body tried to come to terms with having finally *stopped*, part of her brain observed that her originally green dress was now the exact same shade as the ground, somewhere between yellow and brown and desert, and if her hands were anything to judge by, her skin and hair were probably much the same color. If she laid down and closed her eyes, she might just disappear entirely.

She wondered if anyone would notice.

Edward, her husband, probably would. Eventually. When his stomach was screaming for food and nobody was there to mend his clothes or warm his bed at night.

At least they were finally here. Cave Creek, Nevada, the town that would make Edward rich, a place of opportunity and possibility. Edward claimed this would be the end of their misery, and the beginning of their new, better, richer life.

Rose hadn't been of the opinion that their lives back in Arizona were so horrible or poor. In fact, she'd been quite content with meeting her neighborhood friends behind the smithy when their chores were done for the day, and with her job mending clothes for the town's best seamstress. She'd been learning, getting ready to set up her own shop once she had enough money saved. And sewing some baby clothes in private, while Edward was out working the corn fields.

Some day they'd come in handy. And she'd be ready.

Who knew, maybe this barren and forbidding place could be a good town to raise a child. Once they got the town going, that was. Right now it was nothing but a short Main Street that only deserved the name because it was the only street, with two saloons, one general store, and one enormous beautiful hotel.

That hotel was the only thing to convince Rose her husband was perhaps right about this place having a future. If someone rich decided it was worth it to build such grand things, surely they knew something she didn't and were confident more people would flock to the town over time.

Rose certainly hoped they would. She needed new friends.

And a place to sleep tonight.

The land she was sitting on, this dry, rocky blight, was her new home. Edward claimed the land the minute he could meet with the mayor of Cave Creek and introduce himself. Now he was off sticking poles into the ground to mark his territory. She wouldn't be surprised if he marked them like a dog would while he was at it.

As if someone would come during the night and stake a counter-claim.

According to the mayor, this area would be part of the town center soon enough. Edward didn't want to live on Main Street but also had no interest in a larger plot farther out. He'd had enough farming to last him a lifetime, he said, and would make his fortune in the mines around Cave Creek. The mayor had also set him up with a couple of men who supposedly could help him out with getting the equipment he needed and a foot inside a mine.

Rose would leave him to it, and take care of their home to the best of her ability.

At least the view was nice. Rolling foothills down to a large, open valley, and tall, imposing mountains in the distance. Rose had always liked gazing toward faraway places while she cooked or washed clothes or any other chore that didn't demand her eyes to be on it at all times, and she figured if she could look out at this vista while she washed her dishes…maybe it wouldn't be so bad.

With such positive thoughts in mind, she groaned and yelped as she pushed herself into an upright position, stretching her back and shaking out her legs. The worst was done. Now she

It was more of an oval than a circle, really. On the outside, the hot, dry October afternoon. On the inside, coolness and blackness.

Except it wasn't perfectly black. Only dark. As if it was nighttime.

Not daring to go any closer, Rose stayed at two feet and leaned in, narrowing her eyes as she tried to make out shapes inside the darkness. She could have sworn that thing on the right was a table with two chairs pulled up. There was a slight sheen that could come from light reflecting off a smooth surface. And if that was so…

The moon. Outside a window.

Her mind tried to make sense of it as her eyes took in the mountains the moon was hanging on, looking oddly familiar.

She turned check over her shoulder. The same mountains.

Was it a painting? How was it even poss—

The circle wasn't dark anymore.

She was looking into somebody's kitchen, and a beautiful one at that. The table wasn't in the same spot as earlier, this one was on the left, and with four chairs instead of two. The window was in the same spot and offered the same view.

Those same mountains she knew were still behind her, but in daytime, with the sun just coming up in the east. Behind her, it would set in the west in an hour or two.

There was a peacefulness to the room that made her want to step through the circle and pull out a chair. It felt like a home, a good one.

Her foot was halfway to the circle when the image shifted again.

The same kitchen—except the cabinets were blue where they had been red moments before—the same view out the window. And a young woman, perhaps in her thirties, wearing tight-fitting pants of all things and a flimsy blouse that was shockingly see-through. Although Rose knew she had never met this woman before, there was something familiar about her. Something in her eyes and the way she held herself.

The woman glanced up. Her eyes widened as she looked from Rose to the open ground and the mountains behind her and back to Rose.

Rose raised a hand and waved, not certain what the right etiquette was in this case.

Were they not the first to claim the land after all?

The woman was talking to her but no sound came through the circle. She was also making exaggerated gestures. She wanted Rose to stay put.

Rose nodded in acknowledgment.

When she was sure Rose wouldn't come through the circle, the woman ran to the kitchen counter to get a sheet of paper and a small stick. She proceeded to write on the paper with the stick, and held it up toward Rose.

One-way portal. Do not ever go through. The word "ever" was underlined three times.

Rose had no idea what to say to that. A portal? To where?

The woman ran to the kitchen counter again. Lifted a lever, and clear water poured out of a curved pipe.

Plumbing? In such a small house in the middle of nowhere? What kind of magic was this?

The woman pointed to a board on the wall by the door. It said February 13th 1954.

As in, the year, 1954?

The woman scribbled something on her paper again and held it up for Rose to read.

Nice to meet you, Rose. You'll love Cave Creek. Do not tell Edward about our meeting.

The image shifted. The same location. Different…time? She had the view of the inside of a tent. Building materials were sticking out from under the flaps. A house under construction, perhaps?

"What are you doing, just standing around like that, doing nothing?" Edward appeared from behind the bushes hiding the portal from view from most directions. His sharp gaze went to the circle. "What is that?"

"It appears to be a portal?"

Two

Edward watched two scenes—neither had people in them—before deciding they had to protect the portal. Hide it, so nobody would try to take it from them.

"That thing is worth more than a gold mine," he said, that gleam he'd developed over the last year in his eye, the one that made Rose shut up rather than speak up because she didn't know how he'd react to her disagreeing with him.

She agreed on the portal being a gold mine—but probably not in the same sense as Edward.

It was a view into the future. Or *a* future. A view into various families' lives, families that clearly didn't mind having strangers peeking in on them from time to time. They seemed used to it.

While Edward spent all his time building their house, growling at the neighbors dropping by to introduce themselves, thinking they were here to steal his riches, Rose did all her chores inside the tent with the portal. While she prepared their food, she kept an eye on the portal, when she mended their clothes, she'd keep it in her peripheral vision so she could look up if there was movement.

Because *every* time someone was there, they greeted her. They all knew her, apparently by name. Some looked happily shocked to see her, as if they'd been granted a gift. Some appeared worried for her, continually glancing around the tent, looking for something.

Or someone.

The situation was quite different when Edward was present, usually only late at night. He didn't stay awake for long, having used all his energy on building the house around them, but while he was, his greedy eyes were on the portal, more focused on the objects than the people.

"Some of those places have machines that would be worth a fortune," he mumbled into his food one night, while the portal was showing an empty and dark kitchen. "You see that young man the other day who shaved with a black stick over the sink? Didn't even need to be careful not to cut himself."

Rose wondered if the people on the other side detected this unlawful side of Edward, if that was why they pretended not to see them when he was around. They'd glance at the portal, see Edward, and go back to their daily life. If Rose was alone, they'd try to communicate with her. Smiling, waving. Telling her not to come through.

If they already knew Rose's name, maybe they already knew Edward's too.

And they chose not to communicate with him.

Which might explain why Rose didn't tell him about the first woman's warning. That the portal was one-way. It might not be true, of course, but Rose was tempted to believe her.

And Edward was planning on going through to steal the nice people's things.

She should tell him, of course. He was her husband and she would be lost without him. It was her duty to look after his well-being, like he looked after hers. But it would mean trying to explain that the people *could* see them, that they were choosing to ignore them whenever Edward was present. And it would mean trusting he'd believe her when she said the portal was one-way.

She didn't actually *know* this, she only had the first woman's scribbled words. But she believed her. The woman seemed genuinely worried Rose would come through, and it wasn't because she was worried about theft.

Rose just didn't think Edward would believe her if she told him. In fact, he'd most likely become angry and accuse her of trying to hold him back, of taking anybody else's side but his.

Like he'd done when Rose had defended their new neighbors, the Johnsons, saying they were just coming over to be nice. They even brought some type of plant that they claimed could grow in this inhospitable climate, offering it as a welcome gift.

Edward was of the opinion they used the plant as an excuse to spy on his portal.

Rose thought they were trying to be nice and offered to mend their clothes for free the next time they needed it.

The bruises on Rose's arms from his "words" following that discussion cemented her decision not to give any information about the portal.

One of the women on the other side saw the bruises. Rose didn't like the pity she saw in her familiar brown eyes, but she thought she could read lips well enough to understand what she said: "You'll be all right." Which she appreciated.

Even though there was nothing anybody could do because nobody would go through the portal, it felt good to have someone watch over her, worry about her. It meant she still existed, that she wasn't invisible.

One day, she saw a poor, depressed old man, sitting in a sofa in his kitchen. It was the first time she'd seen a sofa in any of the timelines. He had a plate filled with food in his lap and when he appeared in her circle, he looked up quickly, blue eyes searching Rose's side.

At first, he seemed disappointed not to find what he searched for. Then came the usual recognition. Sinking back into his seat, he gave her a nod, and started eating.

Rose enjoyed the companionship.

When it came time to build the kitchen, they had the general structure of the house around it, so they could remove the tent. The portal was no longer visible from outside. They discovered that by bringing the planks in from the back of the portal, they could have the floor at the exact same height as the houses on the other side of the portal. Edward accepted to set up the window in the same spot at the mirror houses, and did a fairly decent job of imitating the general layout of the room.

Rose helped Edward with the building, of course. Because of the portal, he wouldn't let anyone else work on the inside of his house, and he couldn't do everything alone. Rose didn't mind. She was strong and hale and enjoyed learning new things and pushing her boundaries. You never knew when carpenter skills could come in handy in the future.

At times she did have trouble with certain tasks, though. She tired quicker than usual, kept forgetting where she'd put her shears, and couldn't keep her breakfast down most mornings, so often opted to go without. Which made her light-headed.

Edward grumbled, accusing her of avoiding her part of the workload. Rose apologized profusely, hoping it would appease him, but it had the opposite effect.

"You think that just because you prance around here with your pretty smile, I'm going to do all the work? You really think I'm that stupid?"

He gave Rose a hard shove, making her fall to the floor mere inches from the portal. The family on the other side sat still as statues, clearly worried she'd fall through and watching out of the corner of their eyes, but equally intent on not letting Edward know they could see him.

It was seeing the little boy on the other side, with his face full of colorful food because he insisted on eating by himself, that made the information click in her mind.

She was pregnant.

Her body seemed to have come to the same conclusion as

her mind: she was home and it was safe to start a family. What she'd been hoping for since the very first day of her marriage had finally happened.

She was going to be a mother.

"You going to stay there staring at nothing all day? How about helping me setting up this blasted kitchen counter you insisted on having! You're the one who's going to be cooking on it. It's no problem for *me* if you have to do it on the floor."

Instead of giving him the good news, Rose rose to her feet. Her head spun a little, but nothing she couldn't handle. Once the house was finished, Edward wouldn't be so stressed out and their life could go back to normal, to the way they were before he heard talk of the easy money in the gold mines in Nevada.

His conscience simply needed to see to the safety of his family and he'd be easier to live with.

Three

Rose couldn't have been more wrong in her predictions.

Once the house stood ready, Edward became even more agitated and angry. He'd been to see his contacts about working in the mines but it seemed he'd been refused. He didn't even want to work there but needed an explanation for all the riches he was planning of bringing through the portal. No matter what Rose did to appease him, it only made him worse. He'd yell until he became red in the face, shaking his fist at her, the threat of violence very clear.

One night, when a fight erupted in the living room, he made good on the threat. He took Rose's proposition for him to build houses for others now he knew how as criticism to his brilliant plan and drove his fist into her ribs, making her lose her breath for a moment. And her calm.

He could have hurt the baby! Which she still hadn't told him about.

It might have been a coincidence, but Rose noted he had never hit her in the kitchen, where people were potentially watching. He might not know they could see him, but he didn't like having an audience.

He *knew* what he was doing was wrong.

Keeping her tears back, and with a hand to her belly to protect her unborn child, Rose crawled toward the kitchen.

"Where do you think you're going? I'm talking to you!" Edward held up his closed fist again, a clear message.

He didn't expect her to keep going despite his explicit command, though, so Rose made it to the kitchen before he caught up with her.

In the portal, a family of three. A glance at the calendar that all the families had in the same spot revealed it was 1955. A girl of about ten and his parents. Rose had seen them several times already. She liked this bunch. And worried the young girl would have something to do with the sad old man from the sofa.

Rose used the table to pull herself up. Her ribs hurt but she didn't think anything was broken. Her baby should be fine.

As long as Edward didn't hit her again.

"Always staying here in the kitchen," Edward almost spit out. "Looking in on the lives of others instead of taking care of your husband in the here and now. Look at them, sitting there, eating, not even knowing there's an open access into their house. Losers, the lot of them."

What Edward didn't seem to notice was the father in the portal looking directly at him with a fierce frown on his face. One eerily similar to the one on Edward's face.

"I do my best to take care of you," Rose began. "What would you—"

"You're worthless! There's a hole in my shirt and you didn't even notice, let alone fix it."

"Well, if you'd only told me—"

Edward moved toward her. To hit her, to push her, Rose didn't know. But she wasn't letting him risk their baby again. So she stepped away. Closer to the portal.

In her peripheral vision, she saw the woman and the young girl stand up and leave the room. The man went to pick something up from behind a cabinet but Rose couldn't make out what.

"You dare stand up to me?" Edward roared, his face and neck completely red.

Where had her sweet husband gone? Rose hardly recognized the monster in front of her.

He charged her.

Rose acted on reflex. She stepped back, right up to the portal. When Edward's body came within reach, her hands came up to his chest. She used his own momentum to push him aside.

And right through the portal.

His roar cut off abruptly. He fell to the floor in the other kitchen, his dirty clothes oddly out of place in the clean house.

The man stood over him with a baseball bat, ready to swing.

Edward scrambled to his feet. Ran toward Rose.

And bounced right back.

It really was one-way.

Rose barely had the time to meet Edward's shocked eyes before the portal shifted, and she stood looking into a dark, empty kitchen filled with moonlight.

Silence.

Four

Rose couldn't bring herself to leave the kitchen. She kept expecting Edward to come back, to blame her for everything, saying she should have told him the portal was one-way. Punishing her for pushing him through.

But he never came back. The scene in the portal kept shifting as usual, showing different times of day, different years, different families. But never Edward.

The people smiled at her, gave inaudible words of encouragement. And went on with their lives.

Rose fixed dinner. Started painting the kitchen cabinets since the paint was already there and Edward would be mad at her for dallying if he ever made it back. It was the same color as the cabinets of the young woman who had written the warning note.

She set up a sleeping mat in the kitchen. The bedroom was mostly ready but too far from the portal for comfort. If Edward came back, she had to be here to show him the way. Or to make sure he didn't come through—she couldn't quite decide.

Five days after his disappearance he still hadn't come back.

The nice neighbors with the plant dropped by. The man had torn his best suit and wondered if Rose would know how to save it. The woman said she knew how to fix normal tear and wear but didn't trust herself to fix something so expensive.

Rose fixed the suit, and gratefully accepted two chickens as payment.

As she sat in front of the portal, wondering if her chickens were in danger of disappearing into another timeline or if the creatures were perhaps smarter than people when it came to things like this, the scene changed and a woman came into view.

About Rose's size, she had shoulder-length auburn hair and large brown eyes. She seemed to be in her forties, perhaps early fifties. She stood in front of the portal, a large green pack on her back and sturdy shoes on her feet. In her hands, a white cowboy hat and what appeared to be a small blackboard.

When she saw Rose, her eyes lit up. She scribbled something on her board with a piece of chalk.

"Rose Spencer?"

Rose nodded.

The woman wiped the words off the board with the sleeve of her shirt. "Edward gone?"

Another nod.

The woman came through the portal.

"It's one-way!" Rose yelled, her hands reaching toward the woman to help—but how?

"I know." The woman's smile was kind and made the corners of her eyes crinkle. "I was done in that time. This is where I needed to come." She held out her hand toward Rose. "I'm Martha Spencer. I've been wanting to meet you for a long time, Rose."

Rose stared at the outstretched hand. "Spencer?"

Martha kept smiling. "We're all Spencers up until the nineteen nineties or so. I kept my maiden name, but my son carries my husband's name. So from then on, it's mostly Jacksons." Her smile faltered. "There are too many possibilities starting around the turn of the century. The variations in the timelines are great."

Rose shook Martha's hand, not so much out of politeness as of needing it to stop hanging there mid-air. The scene Martha had stepped out of was still there. It would close in a couple of minutes.

"All Spencers," Rose repeated, not sure if it was a question or a statement.

"We're all your descendants," Martha said kindly. "Of the baby you're carrying."

Rose pulled back her hand and retreated across the room, bumping into a chair on the way. Nobody knew about the baby. Not Edward, not the neighbors, not the woman at the grocery store.

"I'm your great-great granddaughter," Martha said, staying where she was like she was dealing with a wild animal. "Or probably the great-great granddaughter of you in a different timeline, but close enough."

Rose had noticed the family resemblance in the various families, of course. Those large brown eyes—Edward's—and the straight-as-an-arrow nose. Had come to the conclusion they were all related, on a subconscious level. But she hadn't extended this logic to herself and the family she was starting.

She'd been an outsider looking in, not part of the group.

"How will you get back to your time?" she asked. It felt safer than all the other questions vying for attention in her mind.

Martha looked down and sighed. "I suspect I won't. I stepped out of my time to save someone. I knew I couldn't go back." Her gaze lifted to meet Rose's. "I don't regret it for a moment. I do miss my husband and my son, but I've come to terms with my role in this family." Her arms raised out to the sides. "I'm the time traveler."

"You've done this for a long time?"

"About ten years in my estimation. It can be difficult to tell how much time has passed when you can't trust the calendars around you, but I've found my system counting days, months and years."

A hand going automatically to her belly, Rose wondered if she would be able to leave her baby behind to save someone else. She hadn't even met him or her yet, and she didn't think she could do it. As for the husband…well, that would depend on the husband, wouldn't it?

"I saw a man in one of the timelines," she said. "He was looking for someone, I think. He looked lonely."

Martha suddenly looked sad. "That's probably my John. I've met others who have also seen him. I ask everyone I meet to write him a note if they ever see him again. But I suspect I will never find my way back to him."

She took a shaky breath. "I saw the future of his timeline once. The portal was boarded up and there was a sign saying there was nobody left. I think John died. I *hope* my beautiful Beau simply left."

Rose had no idea what to say. This woman was either incredibly cold-hearted or incredibly brave. "So you travel through the portal, looking for your family?"

The kind smile made a return. "I travel the portal, helping our family where it's needed. I deliver messages, give financial advice where needed… And I always knew I needed to be here for you. This is where it all starts and nobody wants you to have to do everything by yourself."

"I can take care of myself." If Rose had managed *with* Edward, she could certainly manage without him.

"I know you can. But having a baby can be risky business no matter what time you're from, and I was trained as a doctor in my time before I started my travels. Will you let me stay and make sure your baby is healthy and ready to give us generations of new Spencers?"

The offer did sound tempting. Several of Rose's friends back in Arizona had children and would have given their hard-earned advice, but here she only knew the one woman, and she didn't have children yet. She'd also need to find a way to earn money now that Edward was gone. They were almost at the end of their

Unable to stop it, a tear streaked down Rose's cheek and disappeared into the neckline of her dress. She brushed it away and took a deep breath, nodded. "Thank you. How long will you be staying?"

Martha squeezed Rose's hand before letting go. "As long as you need me, Rose."

Five

With her son William on her lap, Rose waved to the little boy on the other side of the portal. William lifted his pudgy hand too. It might have been a wave, it might have been involuntary—hard to say at his age. The boy on the other side seemed to be four or five and he was staring through the bars of a fence that Martha explained most parents set up while their children were too young to be trusted not to step through time on accident. The boy had his father's blue eyes and the Spencer nose. This was Beau, Martha's little boy.

It was the only timelines she wouldn't stay to observe. Whenever she recognized the kitchen or saw a date from "her" time, she left the house altogether. She claimed it was to protect the people on the other side, so they wouldn't worry about her having stepped through the portal, but Rose was of the opinion the reminders were too hard to bear.

Martha claimed her mission in life was to help the family as a whole, that she was meant to be drawn out of her time so she could travel through timelines, holding them all together, so to speak. Rose wasn't sure she believed in higher powers tearing mothers from their sons. There might be a point to Martha's wandering, but it wasn't only to help Rose in giving life to her boy.

There had to be more.

Which was why she should move on now that Rose was on her feet. The little boy with the blue eyes and the big smile needed her.

Once the vision of Beau disappeared, she would start packing a bag for Martha. She'd need some food, some good clothes, and at least one memento to remember her time with Rose. Something small to fit into the box at the bottom of her backpack. Her memories of all the Spencers she had helped over the years.

Then she would stand vigil with her great-great-granddaughter in front of the portal, until they found a timeline that looked like it might need a helping hand. Or maybe one that would offer some well-deserved rest.

Rose had her healthy boy, her own house, and a growing business as the town's best seamstress. She'd be fine. She would watch over the portal, sending messages across when needed, and watching out for any threats to the family across the centuries.

Keep the family secret.

She was the ultimate matriarch of them all—and she was ready to watch out for them like they had done for her.

AUTHOR'S NOTE

THANK YOU FOR reading *Family Secrets*. I hope you enjoyed it!

This story was written for, and first published in, the Cave Creek anthology, *Bitter Mountain Moonlight*. This anthology contains stories set in the past, written by lots of talented writers, so make sure to check it out.

I have a second story set around the same portal and family. It's turning into a series. The story is called *Moneyline Secrets*. This one was part of the *Open Ended Threat* anthology, the one set in the present.

There's bound to be more stories in this series, so if you like it, make sure you sign up for my newsletter, to make sure you're up to speed on all new publications.

By signing up for my newsletter, you'll also get several free stories, for example the first Ghost Detective short story, *Just Desserts*.

R.W. Wallace
www.rwwallace.com

Also by R.W. Wallace

Mystery

Ghost Detective Novels
Beyond the Grave
Unveiling the Past
Beneath the Surface

Ghost Detective Shorts
Just Desserts
Lost Friends
Family Bonds
Common Ground
Till Death
Family History
Heritage
Eternal Bond
New Beginnings
Severed Ties

The Tolosa Mystery Series
The Red Brick Haze
The Red Brick Cellars
The Red Brick Basilica

Short Story Collections
Deep Dark Secrets
A Thief in the Night

Short Stories
Cold Blue Eternity
Hidden Horrors

Critters
Gertrude and the Trojan Horse
First Impressions
Let Them Eat Cake
Out of Sight
Sitting Duck
Two's Company
Like Mother Like Daughter

Time Travel Secrets (short stories)
Moneyline Secrets
Family Secrets

Romance

French Office Romance Series
Flirting in Plain Sight
Hiding in Plain Sight
Loving in Plain Sight

Short Stories
Down the Memory Aisle

Holiday Short Stories
Morbier Impossible
A Second Chance
The Magic of Sharing
The Case of the Disappearing Gingerbread City
The Lucia Crown

Young Adult (short stories)
Unexpected Consequences
The Art of Pretending
First Impressions

ABOUT THE AUTHOR

R.W. WALLACE WRITES in most genres, though she tends to end up in mystery more often than not. Dead bodies keep popping up all over the place whenever she sits down in front of her keyboard.

The stories mostly take place in Norway or France; the country she was born in and the one that has been her home for two decades. Don't ask her why she writes in English—she won't have a sensible answer for you.

Her Ghost Detective short story series appears in *Pulphouse Magazine*, starting in issue #9.

You can find all her books, long and short, all genres, on rwwallace.com.

www.ingramcontent.com/pod-product-compliance
Lightning Source LLC
LaVergne TN
LVHW041602070526
838199LV00046B/2094